The World Is Full of BABIES!

Mick Manning and Brita Granström

A Doubleday Book for Young Readers

Not all eggs are laid in nests.
You were an egg once. Then you
developed inside your mom like this.

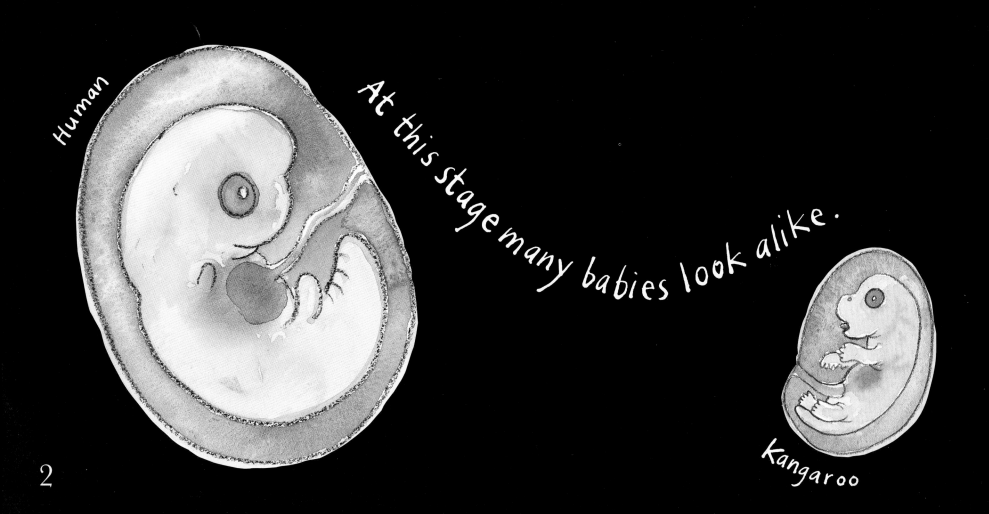

Human

At this stage many babies look alike.

Kangaroo

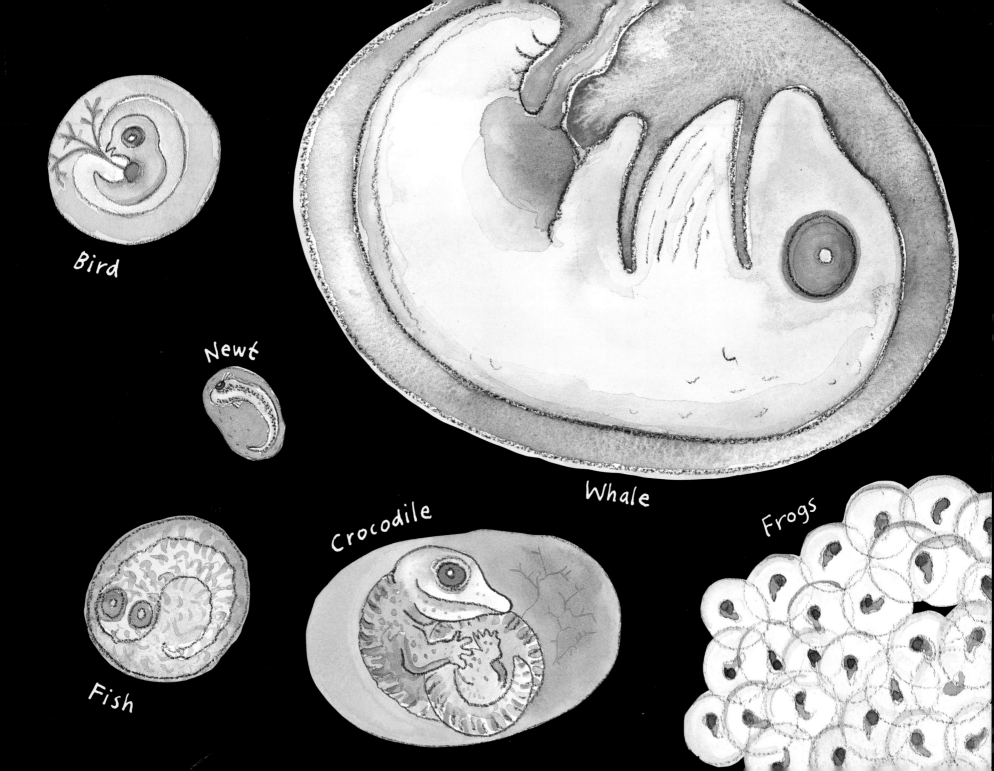

Bird

Newt

Whale

Crocodile

Frogs

Fish

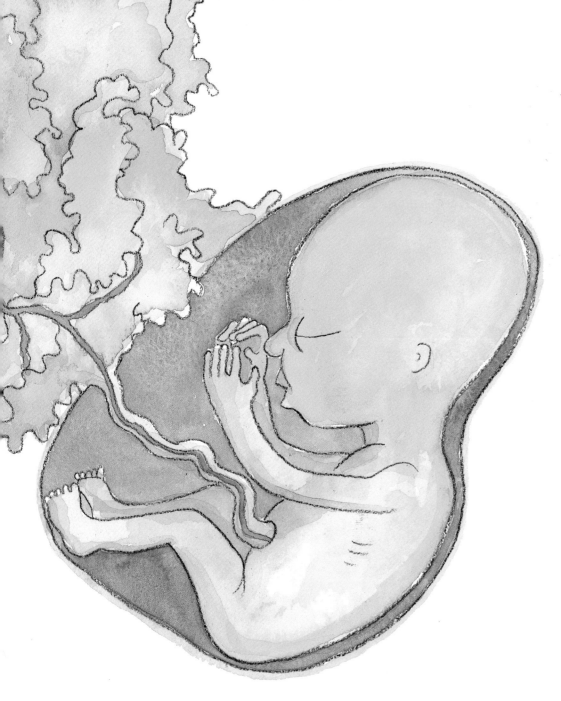

All over the earth, babies are growing.

It took nine months for you to grow big enough to be born.

It takes nine weeks for a puppy to grow and be born.

4

It takes two years for an elephant to grow and be born.

It takes twenty-one days for a house mouse...

All over the earth, babies are being born.

You were born in a warm room.

If you had a cuckoo for a mom, the first thing you would do after you hatched is push all the other eggs out of the nest.

If you had a polar bear for a mom you'd be born in a snow den in the middle of winter.

Maaaaaaaaaahhh!!

All over the earth, babies are crying.
  You often used to cry for your mom.

Parents and babies quickly learn the sounds of each other's voices.

Rhino calves squeal.

Chicks cheep cheep cheep.

Hamsters squeak.

Puppies whimper.

All over the earth, babies are suckling.
You suckled your mom's milk.

Some babies drink milk from a bottle.

Piglets and tiger cubs, monkeys and humans—
all baby mammals drink milk!

If you were a seal pup, you'd drink such rich, fatty milk that you would be three times fatter in just a few days.

All over the earth, babies are sleeping.
You slept cozy in a crib with blankets and
gentle music.

If you were a bat baby
you'd sleep upside down,
hanging on with tiny
fingernails in a drafty
old roof space.

If you were a seabird chick you'd sleep through a storm perched on a cliff high above the sea.

If you were a whale baby you'd float alongside Mom with all the sea for a bed and whale song for a lullaby.

13

All over the earth, babies are being carried around. Perhaps you were carried around outdoors in a sort of baby backpack.

If you were a lemur baby you'd have to hang on tight!

14

All over the earth, babies are growing up.
It took about six months before you
began to crawl across the rug.

But think about this:
If you were a baby rat you would be an
adult in three months with a family
of your own, and you could have twenty
babies every six weeks.
That means three months later you'd
be a grandparent with four hundred
grandchildren.
And three months after that you'd have 8,000 great-grandchildren!

All over the earth, babies are getting dirty!
You couldn't keep yourself clean when you were a baby,
so you wore a diaper and had to be bathed every day.

If you were a kingfisher baby you'd sit happily in a stinking mess of rotten fishbones and droppings!

If you were a cat or a polecat kitten you would be licked clean every day by your mom's rough tongue.

All over the earth, babies are learning to walk. You began to walk at about twelve months.

Many predators are waiting to eat baby animals, so...

If you were a fawn you'd have to be able to jump and run within an hour of being born.

If you were a new butterfly you could take to the air as soon as your wings dried in the sun.

If you were a tiny turtle you'd hurry to the sea as soon as you hatched.

If you were a baby viper you'd be very poisonous.

All over the earth, babies are learning their own language. You started to talk at about two years old. First you said "Mom" or "Dad," then other words came out and you slowly learned to join them together.

If you were a lion cub you'd be learning how to roar.

If you were a honeybee you'd do the "sundance" to show where the best pollen can be found.

If you were an otter you'd learn to whistle.

If you were a wolf cub you'd be learning the howls and calls of your pack.

All over the earth, babies are exploring—
holding hands to stay safe.
Perhaps you still hold Mom's hand.

But if you were part of a shrew family you would hold tails.

All over the earth, babies are playing.
You played hide-and-seek and tag.

Lots of animals play chasing and hiding games
—it's practice for hunting or escaping.

All over the earth, babies are becoming
adults who can have babies of their own.
One day, maybe you will have a baby too.

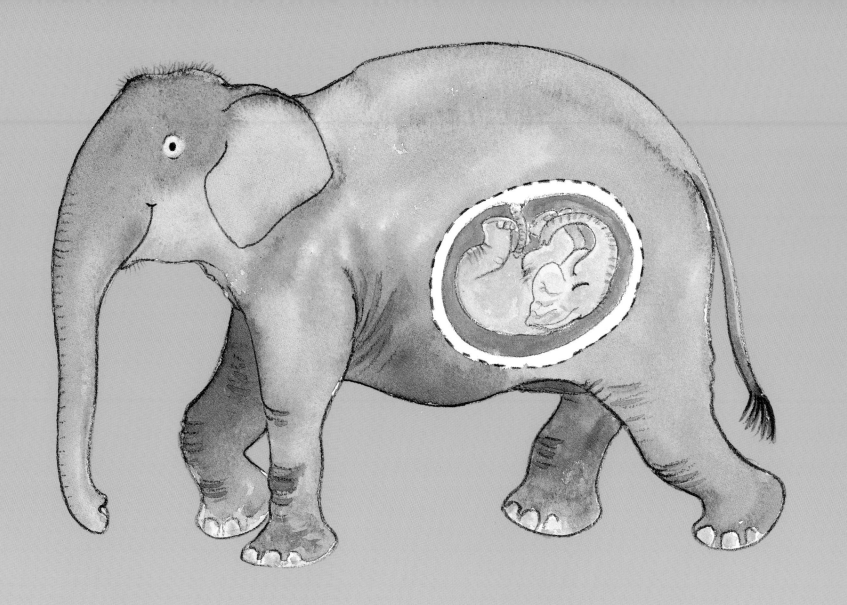

To our parents, with love – MM & BG

A Doubleday Book for Young Readers

Published by
Delacorte Press
Bantam Doubleday Dell Publishing Group, Inc.
1540 Broadway
New York, New York 10036

First published in Great Britain in 1996 by Watts Books, 96 Leonard St., London EC2A 4RH

Library of Congress Cataloging-in-Publication Data

Manning, Mick.
     The world is full of babies! : how all sorts of babies grow and
develop / by Mick Manning and Brita Granström. — 1st American ed.
          p.   cm.
     Originally published: London : Watts, 1995.
     Summary: Presents information about how human babies as well as
many different kinds of animal babies grow and develop from before birth
through early childhood.
     ISBN 0-385-32258-5 (HC : alk. paper)
     1. Infants—Development—Juvenile literature. 2. Animals—
Infancy—Juvenile literature. [1. Babies. 2. Animals—Infancy.]
     I. Granström, Brita. II. Title.
     HQ774.M27 1996
305.23'1—dc20   95-52141
                                                              CIP
                                                               AC

Manufactured in Singapore

The text of this book is set in Baskerville Infant Roman 26-point.
Book design by Mick Manning and Brita Granström

October 1996

10 9 8 7 6 5 4 3 2 1